RETOLD TIMELESS CLASSICS

Tales of the SEVEN WONDERS

Perfection Learning®

Retold by Paula J. Reece

Illustrator: Dan Hatala
Cover and Book Design: Deborah Lea Bell

For information, contact
Perfection Learning® Corporation
1000 North Second Avenue, P.O. Box 500
Logan, Iowa 51546-0500.
Phone: 800-831-4190 • Fax: 712-644-2392

Paperback ISBN 0-7891-5294-0
Cover Craft® ISBN 0-7807-9674-8
Printed in the U.S.A.

3 4 5 6 7 8 PP 08 07 06 05 04 03

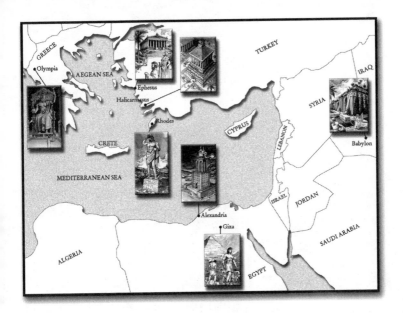

Contents

The LIGHTHOUSE at Alexandria

Only one of the Seven Wonders of the Ancient World had an actual practical purpose. The Lighthouse at Alexandria provided safety for sailors traveling to the Alexandrian harbor. It became the model for similar structures used to "light the way" for ships in the future. In fact, it even became the model for words. The word for "lighthouse" in several languages was derived from the place where that first lighthouse stood—the small island of Pharos. The French word for "lighthouse" is "phare," and the word in Italian and Spanish is "faro."

A baby boy was born in the capital of Macedonia in 356 B.C. However, he wasn't just any ordinary baby boy. Alexander was born to the king of Macedonia and a princess. He was destined to be great. In fact, that became his name—Alexander the Great.

5

When Alexander was 13, his parents decided to hire a tutor for him. They wanted to make sure that he was well educated and skilled. And, of course, they only wanted the best for their son. So they hired Aristotle, a famous Greek philosopher and teacher. He taught Alexander writing, literature, science, medicine, and philosophy.

When Alexander's father died in 336 B.C., Alexander took over the throne. Then he began the greatest conquest of ancient times. He seized kingdom after kingdom. He wanted to spread his empire.

Alexander the Great founded many cities. The most famous and successful of these cities was in Egypt.

"Hmm . . . what can I call this city?" he said aloud to himself. He did his best thinking out loud. "It has to be a name that will make people think of power and greatness. It has to be the best name ever given to a city! Let's see. Power . . . greatness . . . I know! I'll name it after me!"

So he named the city *Alexandria*. He liked the name so much, in fact, that he used it for at least 16 other cities he founded. One can never have too much of a good thing!

Alexander the Great was very careful in choosing the location of his new city in Egypt. He didn't want it built right on the Nile Delta. Instead, he ordered it to be built 20 miles to the west. He didn't want the silt and mud carried by the river to block the harbor.

Alexander died before the city was finished. So Ptolemy, the new ruler of Egypt, finished it.

The city became very rich. Its harbor made trading easy. But the harbor was so busy that it was becoming dangerous. The city needed something to guide the ships into the harbor. But what?

Ptolemy thought and thought. Then, suddenly, a light went on. A lighthouse! That was it!

He would have it built on the connected island of Pharos, which was on one side of the harbor.

Ptolemy knew just the architect for the job. He called for Sostrates.

When Sostrates arrived, he had no idea what type of building Ptolemy wanted.

"Sostrates," began Ptolemy, "I have a project for you. It's not just any project, however. When it is completed, it will be the largest building in the world."

Sostrates opened his eyes wide. He took in a gasp of air. He couldn't believe it. He was wishing for a project of greatness—a way to make his mark in the world. Now, here it was!

"What kind of building will it be?" Sostrates asked the ruler.

"It will be a lighthouse," said Ptolemy.

Sostrates' eyes lit up. All sorts of ideas flashed in his head. He couldn't wait to begin.

Some time later, Ptolemy visited Sostrates. He asked about his progress on the lighthouse.

"Can you describe your plans to me?" asked Ptolemy.

"I'd be happy to," said Sostrates. "The lighthouse will be about 380 feet high. It will be made of marble blocks. Lead mortar will hold the bricks together. There will be three sections. Each will be on top of the other."

"What will each section be like?" asked Ptolemy.

"The lowest section will be shaped like a large box," said Sostrates. "It will be about 200 feet high. I've planned hundreds of storage rooms inside."

"The second section," he continued, "will be an eight-sided tower. On top of the tower will be a cylinder that extends up to an open cupola. That's where the fire will burn. On top of the cupola will stand a large statue of the god Poseidon. The inside of the upper two sections will have a shaft. A small elevator will be installed to take the fuel up to the fire. That's also where the mirror will be."

"Mirror?" asked Ptolemy. "What will that be used for?"

"The large, curved mirror will be used to project the light from the fire into a beam," Sostrates explained.

People all over the ancient world were fascinated with the story of the mirror. It was reported that ships could see the light or the smoke from the fire, day or night. And from up to 100 miles away!

Other stories described how the mirror was used as a weapon. Legend says that it could be used to concentrate the light from the sun and burn enemy ships as they approached. One report even claimed that by using the mirror, it was possible to see what was going on in the city of Constantinople—far across the sea!

It took 20 years for the first lighthouse in the world to be completed. By this time, Ptolemy was dead. Sostrates was extremely proud of his work. The lighthouse was a marvelous sight! So Sostrates approached the new ruler, Ptolemy II, about getting his name on the building.

"Sir," Sostrates began, "I have dedicated 20 years of my life to this lighthouse. I would like my name to be engraved on it so everyone will remember my work."

"I'm sorry," said Ptolemy II, "but I want my name to be the only one on the lighthouse. You will carve mine and no other."

Sostrates was angry. But he didn't dare tell Ptolemy II that. He just came up with his own secret plan. You see, Sostrates was a very clever man.

Sostrates called over one of his trusty workers. He explained what he wanted the worker to do.

"I have an inscription I want you to chisel into the foundation," Sostrates said. He wanted it to say

SOSTRATES, THE SON OF DEXIPHANES, THE CNIDIAN, DEDICATED THIS TO THE SAVIOUR GODS, ON BEHALF OF THOSE WHO SAIL THE SEAS.

"Then," Sostrates continued, "I want you to cover the words with plaster. Then chisel 'Ptolemy II' into only the plaster."

Sostrates' cleverness paid off. For as the years went by, the plaster aged. And as it did, it chipped away. And it revealed Sostrates' inscription!

The lighthouse attracted visitors from all over. An observation deck was at the top of the first level. Tourists could buy food and enjoy the view. Brave visitors could climb to the top of the eight-sided tower for an even better view. The ancient world didn't provide many opportunities to see the world from such a perspective.

The lighthouse stood for many centuries. It became so famous that it was shown on Roman coins. The lighthouse was damaged during several earthquakes. It was finally demolished in an earthquake around 1326 A.D.

The Hanging GARDENS

of Babylon

*Travelers in the desert sometimes think they see
lush oases in the midst of the dry sand. However,
most of these turn out to be mere mirages. But not
in the case of King Nebuchadnezzar II in Babylon.
He created a true oasis—a hanging paradise—as a
gift for his wife.*

Once upon a time in the city of Babylon there
lived King Nebuchadnezzar II and his wife, Amyitis.
The two had been married as part of a treaty. It
brought together the nations of the two young people.

Queen Amyitis had grown up in Media. There,
the land was green and rugged. She always had a
view of the mountains. It was beautiful.

13

But then Amyitis got married. And she had to move to Babylon.

One day Queen Amyitis sat looking out the window of her palace.

"I'm so depressed," she told her husband.

"But why, my dear?" King Nebuchadnezzar asked. "We're one of the most powerful empires in the world."

"I know," Amyitis said. "But it doesn't matter. There is no beauty here. The sun has baked the land. It's flat and brown."

King Nebuchadnezzar looked out the window too. He had grown up in Babylon. So the flat, dry land didn't bother him. He was used to it.

"I wish it would rain," Amyitis said. "It never rains! I wish to see green plants and hills. I miss my home."

"I'm sorry, my queen," King Nebuchadnezzar said. "I didn't realize the move was so difficult for you."

"My eyes just long to gaze at some beauties of nature," she said.

Now King Nebuchadnezzar was a very clever man and king. He was already making great improvements in the city. So he began to develop an idea.

"If I can't take my wife to the mountains," he said, "then I will bring the mountains to her."

King Nebuchadnezzar then called in architects and engineers. "I have decided to build my wife an artificial mountain with rooftop gardens," he announced.

At first, the engineers and architects thought King Nebuchadnezzar had lost his mind. This was mainly because it rarely rained in Babylon. How did the king think he would get flowers and plants to survive?

But the king was very smart. And he had a vivid imagination. He had already envisioned the plan for his "hanging gardens."

"We will use irrigation to water the plants," King Nebuchadnezzar told the engineers.

"Where will the water come from?" one engineer asked.

"It will come from the nearby Euphrates River," the king answered.

"But how will we get the water from the river to the plants?" another engineer asked.

The king explained. "Water will be lifted far into the air," he said. "Then it will flow down through terraces that will be built and water the plants at each level. The terraces will be made of baked brick and asphalt."

"But how will we lift the water?" asked yet another confused engineer.

"We will use what is called a 'chain pump,' " the king said. "Have any of you heard of this?"

A few of the engineers timidly raised their hands.

"Very well," continued the king. "Allow me to explain. A chain pump has two large wheels. One is above the other, and they are connected by a chain. The bottom wheel will be situated above the river. Buckets are hung on the chain. As the bottom wheel is turned, the buckets will dip into the pool. They will pick up the water. The chain will then lift them to the upper wheel. There, the buckets will be tipped and dumped into a pool of water at the top of the terraces. The chain will then carry the empty buckets down to be refilled. The water at the top of the terraces will be released by gates into channels. These channels will be like artificial streams that will water the gardens."

"Sounds fascinating," said one engineer. "What will power the chain pump?"

"Good question," said the king. "This will be a good job for our slaves. The bottom pump wheel is attached to a handle. Turning the handle generates the power."

Work on the hanging gardens then began.

Tropical plants were planted on the roof of the palace.

The garden stood on huge slabs of stone. The stone was covered with layers of reed, asphalt, and tiles. Sheets of lead were then laid so the water didn't rot the foundation. Then on top of that was placed a large amount of dirt. Enough for the greatest trees to be planted in. Everything was done to ensure that the garden would stay permanently green.

When Queen Amyitis saw the finished gardens, she was awestruck.

"Why, they're beautiful!" she cried as she looked out at the gardens. They were 400 feet wide and 400 feet long. The height was more than 80 feet.

"I'm glad you like it, my dear," said King Nebuchadnezzar. "I'm sorry I couldn't take you to your green hills. But I hope this will remind you of the beauty of your homeland."

Queen Amyitis looked once again at the leafy artificial mountain rising out of the city on the plain.

"Oh, yes," said the queen. "It will. And it will always remind me of the beauty in you."

The Statue of ZEUS at Olympia

From the town of Olympia emerged a tradition to which it gave its name—the Olympic Games. The Olympian god Zeus oversaw the sacred event. When it was time to build a sculpture honoring their god, the Olympians called on Phidias. And like Michelangelo painting the Sistine Chapel, Phidias took his task very seriously.

"Let the games begin!" went the cry at the first Olympic Games.

It was 776 B.C. The creation of city-states in Greece had encouraged competition among the citizens. The games began as a way to bring honor to one's city-state. And also as a way to honor the god Zeus.

Battles and wars were set aside during the time of the games. The Olympics was not just an athletic event—it was a sacred festival.

The site of the games included a stadium and a sacred grove that housed temples. In this grove stood a shrine to Zeus. Near the temple grew a wild olive tree. Its branches were used to make the wreaths for the winners to wear.

At first, the Temple of Zeus was very simple. But as time went by and the Olympic Games became more popular, the people of Olympia knew that something more had to be done.

So around 470 B.C., a man named Lisbon of Elis was asked to create a new temple.

"I will design a temple worthy of our king of gods," he said. His masterpiece was finished in 456 B.C.

The new temple was built on a raised platform. The roof was supported by 13 columns on the sides and 6 on each end. Sculptures were carved into the stone. It was thought to be one of the best examples of architectural design.

Yet the people of Olympia were not satisfied.

"It's stately . . . but it doesn't seem to be enough," said one Olympian leader.

"Yes, it does seem to need something more," said another. "The temple alone doesn't seem worthy of Zeus. But what else can we do?"

"I know!" said another citizen. "What about building a statue in the temple?"

"Yes," everyone agreed, "that is exactly what the temple needs."

The leaders of Olympia were careful in choosing just the right sculptor for the job. It wasn't just any ordinary statue he would be building. It was a tribute to the most important god of all.

Finally the leaders decided on a man named Phidias.

"He has built a 40-foot statue of the goddess Athena for the Parthenon in Athens," one leader explained.

"And he has worked on the outside of the temple too," said another.

Phidias was then summoned to come to Olympia. He would be building the most important sculpture of his life—the Statue of Zeus.

When Phidias arrived, he set up a workshop. It was just west of the temple. And he put all of his energy into designing and building the sacred statue.

"It has to be very special," he said to himself.

"It can't be made of just ordinary stone." So Phidias designed the statue using some very precious materials.

"And it has to be very large," he said.

And large it was. When it was finished, the statue was 40 feet tall and was 22 feet wide!

The people of Olympia were anxious to view this new wonder. As they filed through the temple, they saw that Zeus was seated on an elaborate throne. And his head nearly touched the roof!

Reactions to the size of the figure were mixed.

"How can Zeus be seated with his head nearly touching the roof?" some asked as they looked at the statue. "If he stood up, he would crash through the temple. The proportions are all wrong."

But others thought differently. "The statue represents Zeus's size and power," they said. "It makes him seem larger than life, which he is."

In its right hand, the statue held the figure of Nike, the goddess of victory. In its left hand, the statue held a scepter that was topped with an eagle.

Zeus's skin was made of ivory. His beard, hair, and robe were made of gold.

But the throne was the most impressive of everything. It was made out of gold, ebony, ivory, and precious stones. Figures of Greek mythology were carved into the chair.

So Phidias was hailed as the sculptor of the greatest statue of the times. Life was good for Phidias. That is, until he returned home.

You see, Phidias had a close friend named Pericles. Pericles ruled Athens and had many enemies. His enemies weren't able to attack him directly. So instead, they attacked his friend.

Phidias was accused of stealing gold that was meant for the statue of Athena. But it couldn't be proven. So the enemies of Pericles thought of something else.

They claimed that he had carved his own image and the image of Pericles into a sculpture on the Parthenon. The Greeks considered this very improper. So Phidias was thrown in jail. Sadly, he died awaiting his trial.

But the statue of Zeus Phidias had created survived for centuries. It remained at the temple in Olympia until 225 A.D. That's when the Olympic Games were abolished by the emperor of Rome. He thought that the games were anti-Christian.

So the statue was moved by wealthy Greeks to the city of Constantinople. It remained there until 462 A.D., when it was destroyed in a fire.

The Temple of Artemis

Most buildings today pale in comparison to the architecture of the ancient world. Such is the case with the last monumental temple dedicated to the goddess Artemis. It was the first building to be made completely of marble, a very precious material then and today. Some of the many columns and statues were made by the most famous artists of the time. What's left of this marvel today? Is there anything left to remind us of the wonder of the past? Just one single column in the middle of a marshy field.

"I think we're lost," said the crusader leader. "This doesn't look like the great city of Ephesus."

It was 1100 A.D. A group of crusaders was traveling across Asia Minor. The leader wanted to stop at a great city and port he had read about in ancient texts. It sounded marvelous.

"I read that this was a large seaport city," said the leader. "It was said to have many ships docked in the bay."

"Well, sir," said another crusader, "the sea is nearly three miles away."

"Yes," said another, "there are no ships to be seen. And we are standing in a swamp."

Looking around, the leader noticed a man a few hundred feet away. He was sitting in front of a small, crumbling building. He was gazing off toward the sea.

"Let's ask him where we are," said the leader, pointing to the stranger.

The crusaders approached the man, who barely took his eyes off the horizon of the sea.

"Excuse me, sir," said the leader, "but could you please tell me if this is the city of Ephesus?"

The man looked up. "It was once called that," he said. "But now it is named Ayasalouk."

"But where is your bay?" asked the leader. "Where are your trading ships? And where is the magnificent Greek temple that we have heard of?"

The stranger looked confused. "Temple? What temple?" he asked. "We have no temple here, sir."

Now the leader was confused. He thanked the man for his time and led his men away.

"I just don't understand," said the leader to his crusaders. "Could all the reports of this glorious temple be lies?"

Just then another strange man approached the group of crusaders. "Excuse me," he said. "I couldn't help overhearing your conversation. I think I can help you."

"But who are you?" asked the leader.

Said the stranger, "I am one of the few who remembers."

"Please, sit down," said the leader. "We are all curious. Please share with us what you know."

So the stranger sat with the crusaders on the damp, sandy ground. "The town that once admired the Greek temple with such pride has now forgotten it," said the stranger. "But I won't. And I want to tell you so others remember too."

"The temple went through many changes before it was destroyed," the stranger continued. "It was first built probably around 800 B.C. It was built as a shrine to the Greek goddess Artemis."

"Didn't it have a sacred stone?" asked the leader.

"You have read up on this," said the stranger. "Yes, it did have a sacred stone. It was a stone that fell from the sky. Over the next 200 years, this temple was destroyed and rebuilt several times."

"Then what happened?" asked another curious crusader.

"Well," said the stranger, "by 600 B.C. Ephesus had become a major trading port. An architect named Chersiphron was hired to build a new temple. High stone columns were part of his design."

"How did they carry the columns to the temple site?" asked the leader.

"The architect was afraid that if the columns were carried in carts, those carts could get stuck in the swampy ground around the site," the stranger explained. "So he laid the columns on their sides and had them rolled to where they would be erected."

"A clever man," said one crusader.

"Unfortunately, this temple didn't last long either," continued the stranger. "In 550 B.C. Ephesus was captured by King Croesus. The temple was destroyed during the fighting."

"How sad," said the leader.

"Yes, but King Croesus felt bad about the temple," said the stranger. "He paid for a new temple to be built there."

"Was that temple just like the others?" asked a crusader. He had been silent, but now he was becoming very interested in the story.

"Not at all," said the stranger. "This one dwarfed the ones that had been built before."

"How big was it?" asked the leader.

"It was 300 feet long and 150 feet wide," answered the stranger. "Its area was four times the size of the previous temple. It took more than 100 stone columns to support its roof. The people of Ephesus took great pride in it until 356 B.C. That's when tragedy struck."

"Tragedy?" asked one of the crusaders.

"Tragedy," repeated the stranger. "And his name was Herostratus."

"Who was this Herostratus?" asked the leader.

"Herostratus was a young man," explained the stranger. "And more than anything he wanted to have his name go down in history."

"What did he do?" asked another crusader.

"He burned the temple to the ground," said the stranger sadly.

"What happened to him?" asked the leader. "Surely he was punished."

"Yes, indeed," said the stranger. "The people of Ephesus were very angry. So angry that they made a law that anyone who spoke of Herostratus would be put to death."

"So much for having his name go down in history," said the leader.

"Was another temple built?" asked a crusader.

"Another architect was hired to build yet another temple," said the stranger. "By this time, Ephesus was one of the greatest cities in the land. No expense was spared in the construction."

"What was this one like?" asked the leader.

"First, layers of charcoal were laid to prepare the ground," described the stranger. "Then fleeces of wool were placed on top of that. The building was made completely of marble—the first of its kind."

"How big was this one?" asked a crusader.

"It was 425 feet long and 225 feet wide," answered the stranger. "It took 127 columns that were each 60 feet high to support the roof. Some of the columns even had figures carved into them."

"Amazing!" said the leader of the crusaders. "How long did this project take?"

"Some say it took 120 years," said the stranger.

"Others argue that it only took half that time. But either way, it took quite a long time."

"When Alexander the Great came to Ephesus in 333 B.C., the temple was still being built," continued the stranger. "He said he would pay for completing the temple if the city would credit him as the builder. The city leaders didn't want Alexander's name carved on the temple. But they were too afraid to tell him."

"What did they do?" asked the leader.

"Finally the city leaders told Alexander, 'It is not fitting that one god should build a temple for another god,' " said the stranger. "This fed Alexander's ego so much that he didn't mention it again."

The stranger paused for breath. He took a drink from a flask and then continued.

"The architect had a problem with a large beam he had to put into position above the door," the stranger continued. "He couldn't find a way to get it to lie flat. It was crooked. He worried and worried until one night when he had a dream. In his dream, the goddess Artemis herself appeared. She told him not to worry. She had moved the stone beam to the proper position. The next morning the architect found that the beam had, indeed, settled into its proper place."

The crusaders' eyes were wide with amazement. The story of the temple was becoming more fantastic with every word. But the crusaders knew that the stranger told the truth.

"So what happened to this great temple?" asked the leader after a pause.

"Christianity came to the region," explained the stranger. "The temple was destroyed by invaders in 262 A.D. By that time, the city was in decline. The new Christians didn't want to rebuild the temple."

"What happened to the city?" asked the leader of the crusaders.

"Silt from the river filled the bay," said the stranger. "Ships could no longer dock. Ephesus wasn't important for trade anymore. In the end, what remained of the city was miles from the sea. Many people left the swampy lowland to live in the surrounding hills."

The stranger stopped then and looked at the crusaders.

"But the temple is still here, in a way," he said.

"Where?" the crusaders asked, looking around.

The stranger pointed to the few buildings that were standing in the swampy village.

"There, in those buildings," he said. "The people who remained here used the ruins of the temple for building materials. Many beautiful sculptures were pounded into powder to make lime for wall plaster."

The crusaders looked around at the run-down buildings. And in their place they tried to picture the magnificence of the Temple of Artemis—an architectural wonder.

The MAUSOLEUM *at* Halicarnassus

Little did Queen Artemisia know that when she commissioned a tomb to be built for her husband, it would cause his name to go down forever in history. And for more than one reason. For one, his stately tomb is known as one of the Seven Wonders of the World. And the name of King Mausolus is forever enshrined in the English word for a large tomb—"mausoleum."

Queen Artemisia's husband was dead. She could barely force herself to say the word.

"Come, Your Majesty," said Queen Artemisia's faithful servant. "You must not give in to despair."

35

Queen Artemisia had fallen into the depths of sadness after her husband, King Mausolus, died.

"But I can't stop thinking about what a great man he was," cried Queen Artemisia. "He ruled over Halicarnassus for 24 years. He brought Greek culture to the area. What a tragedy it is that such a great man is gone."

"It is very sad," said her servant, "that is true. But such grieving is not good for you. You must think of a positive way to remember the great king."

"Yes, you are right," said the queen. "I will think of something."

So Queen Artemisia began thinking of a way to remember her husband. She wanted to make sure no one forgot what a wonderful king he had been.

She thought of many different ideas. But none seemed worthy of the king.

Finally Queen Artemisia knew who could help her. So she went to the king himself—his burial chamber, that is.

"Oh, my husband, my king!" cried Queen Artemisia. "I long to pay you the tribute you deserve. But I cannot find a project that is worthy of your excellence."

The queen looked around the burial chamber. "What a drab place this is," she said. "It's a shame that you will have to spend all eternity here."

Suddenly the queen got an idea. "That's it!" she cried. "Oh, my lord, I will pay you the tribute you deserve. I now know what I must do!"

The queen quickly left. Then she called for her messengers.

When the messengers arrived, Queen Artemisia informed them of their duty.

"Men, you have a very important job," she began. "I am sending you to Greece. My husband was so fond of that land. There, I want you to find and bring me the most talented artists."

The messengers knew not to ask any questions. They received their instructions and then left for Greece.

When the messengers returned some time later, they brought with them hundreds of men. One of them was Scopas. He had supervised the rebuilding of the Temple of Artemis. Other famous sculptors also arrived, along with many other craftsmen.

After all the artists had gathered in the castle, the queen explained her plan.

"Your duty," she began, "will be to build the most exquisite tomb in the world. Anything less will not be good enough for my late husband. I will spare no expense!"

So the artists were off. They began designing the most elaborate burial tomb ever.

It was decided that the tomb would be built on a hill overlooking the city. When the artists had brainstormed some ideas, they again met with Queen Artemisia.

"Tell me what you have come up with," the queen told the artists. "But remember, it had better be good."

Scopas stepped forward and began to describe their plans. "My queen, we see the tomb as being set in an enclosed courtyard," he began.

The queen thought for a moment. "Yes," she said. "I like that. Go on."

The artist became more confident. "And," he continued, "the tomb will sit on a stone platform. On either side of a staircase leading up to the platform will be stone lions."

"Majestic lions for a majestic king," said Queen Artemisia. "Very fitting. Please continue."

"The outer wall of the platform will be adorned with statues," said Scopas. "The statues will represent gods and goddesses. And on each corner of the platform will stand stone warriors and horses."

"To guard the king," said the queen. "That is very comforting. Wonderful plans so far."

Scopas continued. "The tomb will be set in the center of the platform," he said. "It will be made of marble."

"How will the tomb be decorated?" asked the queen.

"The tomb will be a relief sculpture," said Scopas. "It will show different action scenes from Greek mythology and history."

"My husband did admire the Greeks," Queen Artemisia reminisced. "What else?"

"On top of the tomb will perch 36 columns," Scopas said. "A statue will stand in between each column. The roof will be like a stepped pyramid. And on top of that will be the most amazing sculpture of all."

"What is it?" asked Queen Artemisia.

"It is a sculpture of four massive horses pulling a chariot," answered the artist. "In the chariot will be images of King Mausolus and yourself, my queen."

Queen Artemisia was speechless. It would be even more beautiful than she had imagined.

After she gained her composure, the queen thanked the artists.

"Now, hire the builders," she commanded Scopas. "I want construction to begin now."

But the building of the tomb was interrupted soon after it began. For the first time since the death of her husband, Queen Artemisia found herself in a crisis.

"Your majesty, I have just received word that the Rhodians have sent a fleet of ships," panted the queen's advisor as he quickly entered her chambers. "They are heading this way to capture the city!"

Queen Artemisia had been afraid that something like this would happen. King Mausolus had conquered Rhodes, an island in the Aegean Sea. The people of Rhodes, of course, were not happy about it. And now that they knew the king was dead, they thought they could get their revenge.

But the Rhodians had not counted on the cleverness of Queen Artemisia. And her determination to keep everything her husband had worked so hard for. For Queen Artemisia had a plan—a good plan.

The queen sent her own ships to hide in a secret location. After the troops went ashore from the Rhodian fleet of ships, Queen Artemisia's fleet made a surprise raid. They captured the Rhodian ships. Then they towed them out to sea!

But Queen Artemisia wasn't finished there. She ordered her own soldiers to board the Rhodian ships and sail them back to Rhodes. Since the Rhodians thought the ships that were returning held their victorious soldiers, they didn't put up a defense. So the city was easily captured by Queen Artemisia's soldiers. The rebellion was stopped.

Queen Artemisia joined her husband only two years after his death. She was buried in the unfinished tomb with him. The artists decided to stay and finish the work in memory of the honorable king and his devoted queen.

The Great
PYRAMID
of Giza

Only one of the Seven Wonders of the World still remains standing today. The Great Pyramid of Giza, along with all the other pyramids in Egypt, has fascinated people for thousands of years. And why wouldn't it? It is nearly impossible to imagine the work it took to build such monstrous structures. Especially in the days when everything was done by hand. When picturing how big the Great Pyramid is, consider this—it is 30 times larger than the Empire State Building, and it is so large that it can be seen from the moon.

43

Ahmose sat quietly on the boat that was floating down the Nile River. He was nervous, yet excited. He was from a small village in Egypt. He farmed there with his family.

Excitement wasn't common for Ahmose. The only thing to look forward to was market day. It brought a couple hundred people to his village. Otherwise, the few people in his town were quiet and kept to themselves. And now that it was flood season, there wasn't much for him to do.

But a few days before, King Khufu's men had arrived. Ahmose had felt his heart beat faster in his chest. What did they want? he wondered. He soon found out.

The king's men looked over the young men in the village. Then the men approached Ahmose.

"We have a project we need your help with," they said.

"Me?" asked Ahmose. He felt proud that the king would think of him as important.

"The king has instructed his people to build a pyramid for him," said one of the king's men. "It will serve as his tomb when he travels to the afterlife."

"We are looking for strong men to help build this pyramid," said another of the king's men.

Ahmose had been scared. What if he couldn't do it? He was used to hard work, but he hadn't had much experience with building.

But Ahmose had also been excited. Finally—a chance to get out of his small village. A chance to see the wonders of Egypt!

And now here he was—floating down the Nile.

A man struck up a conversation with Ahmose on the boat.

"What have you heard about this pyramid?" asked the man.

"Not very much," said Ahmose. "I just know that King Khufu wanted it built for him."

"The king's men estimate they will need about 20,000 men to work on it," said the man.

Ahmose couldn't believe it. He couldn't even picture that many people. He thought that 200 people in his village on market day was a lot!

"It's going to be hard work," the man continued. "We'll be responsible for hauling the stone blocks."

"How much do they weigh?" asked Ahmose.

"Some only weigh about two tons," said the man. "But the ones that will be used as the ceiling of the king's burial chamber could weigh over 40 tons!"

The thought of that much weight made Ahmose's arms and back ache. He now wasn't sure what he had gotten himself into.

"But don't worry," the man continued. "There is a way for us to haul the stones that makes it easier."

"What's that?" asked Ahmose.

"We will haul the stones up ramps," answered the

man. "The ramps are made of mud, stone, and wood. We will do this by using twine."

"Will we have to cut and set the stones ourselves?" asked Ahmose. He was glad that this man was so friendly. He was learning a lot about what his important job would include.

"Oh, no," said the man. "They have skilled laborers who will do that. They are experienced in that type of work."

"Good," said Ahmose. He didn't want to be responsible for the great pyramid toppling over.

The man noticed the worry lines that had been forming on Ahmose's face in the last few minutes.

"Don't worry," the man told Ahmose. "You'll do fine. They have a nice camp set up. Even a bakery for fresh bread."

The man's words made Ahmose feel better. He set his eyes on the horizon. He couldn't wait to see the pyramids. Some were over 100 years old. But Ahmose had never seen them. No one in his village had ever been given a chance to sail like this down the Nile.

Then Ahmose's mind drifted back to his family. He had never been separated from them, either. He wasn't sure how long the king would need him. Months . . . years . . . Suddenly an even more distressing thought came to Ahmose. What if he never saw them again?

"Excuse me," Ahmose said to the man who was still sitting beside him. "But . . . could you tell me how many men are hurt or . . . killed working on this pyramid?"

The man looked hard at Ahmose. "Some men die," he said honestly. "It's backbreaking work. Accidents do occur."

Ahmose looked sadly at the water. The man continued.

"But," he said, "the camps do offer emergency care. Men have been treated for broken hands or legs. And they have survived."

Just then shouts broke out on the boat. Men were standing and pointing at the horizon. Ahmose looked. And then he knew why.

There, on the horizon, he saw what looked to be a giant mountain. But as they drifted closer, he could see that it was made of stone—a pyramid.

Ahmose had closed his eyes many times and tried to imagine what a pyramid looked like. But in his mind it had never looked as magnificent as it did now in real life. His chest swelled with pride when he thought, I will help build a pyramid even greater than this!

Ahmose went on to become one of the thousands of men who helped build the Great Pyramid of Giza. More than 2 million stones were used to give the pyramid a height of 450 feet. The tomb Ahmose helped build was truly fit for a king!

The COLOSSUS
of Rhodes

The Colossus of Rhodes was constructed to celebrate the unity and freedom of the Greek island of Rhodes. The figure wearing a spiked crown was so wondrous that it inspired modern artists, such as French sculptor Auguste Bartholdi. In fact, his most famous sculpture very much resembles the ancient wonder both in appearance and spirit. And it stands guarding a harbor too. What statue is that? You guessed it—the Statue of Liberty.

Where the Aegean Sea and the Mediterranean Sea meet is a little island called Rhodes. In ancient

49

times the island had one of the best natural harbors in the area. So in 408 B.C. a city was built. It was also called Rhodes. It became important for trading in the ancient world.

The little island survived several invasions. But in 332 B.C. it was finally captured by a man named Alexander the Great. However, this leader didn't live very long. In 323 B.C. he died of a fever. He was only 33 years old.

"Now that Alexander is dead, I will control his vast kingdom!" said one of his generals.

"Why should you control it?" asked another. "I have just as much right!"

"Don't forget me," said yet another general. "Alexander would have wanted me to rule his land."

The three generals fought. Those generals were Ptolemy, Seleucus, and Antigous. The fight ended with the kingdom being divided into three parts. Antigous's part included Rhodes.

But all was not well.

"We want Ptolemy! We want Ptolemy!" shouted the people of Rhodes. They had supported Ptolemy during the power struggle. That angered Antigous.

"Demetrius, come here," Antigous called to his son.

"Yes, Father," answered Demetrius. "What is it?"

"Son, I want you to do something for me," said

Antigous. "I am angry at the people of Rhodes. They helped Ptolemy during our fight for Alexander's kingdom. I am sending you to Rhodes. You must punish the city."

"Very well, Father," said his son. "I will do as you wish."

So Demetrius set off for the city of Rhodes. He took with him an army of 40,000 men—more than the entire population of Rhodes. He also recruited pirates of the Aegean Sea to help.

But the people of Rhodes didn't give up.

The city was surrounded by a tall, strong wall.

"How do you suggest we get over that wall?" Demetrius asked one of his advisors.

"I think we should try building a seige tower to climb over it," said the advisor.

"Good idea," said Demetrius.

Seige towers were wooden structures. They had armlike catapults. These could be used to scale a wall.

Some of the seige towers were made to be rolled on land. But Demetrius had a different plan.

"Instead of attacking on land," Demetrius said, "we will attack by sea. We can mount the tower to six ships that are lashed together."

"I think that just might work," said his advisor.

However, luck was not on Demetrius's side. As he was getting ready for attack, a storm erupted. The tower was turned over and smashed. The people of Rhodes won the battle.

However, Demetrius wasn't beaten yet. He instructed that a second "supertower" be built.

"This one will be 150 feet high," he described. "It will have many more catapults than the other. We will cover it with wood and leather to protect the troops inside from flying arrows. This one will even carry water tanks. That way, we can put out any fires that are started by flaming arrows. Since this tower will be on wheels, it can just be rolled up to the wall."

Demetrius's army was sure that nothing could stop this supertower. But the people of Rhodes had a different plan.

The army began rolling the big tower up to the wall. They were ready for attack. Arrows began flying, and soldiers were in position to man the catapults. Everything seemed to be going their way.

Just then the people of Rhodes sent water flooding into a ditch outside the walls. Demetrius hadn't anticipated that. The heavy war machine got stuck in the mud. And to make matters worse, Ptolemy had sent a fleet of ships from Egypt to help the people of Rhodes. Demetrius could see the ships approaching the harbor.

Demetrius quickly fled. He left the great siege tower where it was—stuck in the mud.

The people of Rhodes were so happy to have defeated Demetrius and his army. They were free!

"What should we do to celebrate?" asked one citizen.

Many people had ideas. But one idea stood out from the rest. They would build a giant statue of their patron god Helios.

"What should we use to build the statue?" asked another citizen. No one spoke for a moment. They were all thinking. They looked around. Then they saw the siege tower and many other war machines that Demetrius had left behind.

So the bronze from the war machines was melted down for the statue. And the siege tower was used as the scaffolding while they were building it.

Construction took 12 years. But when it was finally finished, the statue stood 110 feet high. The figure wore a spiked crown. It shaded its eyes from the rising sun with its right hand. It held a cloak over its left hand. It stood on a 50-foot pedestal near the entrance of the harbor. It was spectacular.

The Colossus stood guard over the harbor for only 66 years. A strong earthquake hit Rhodes in 226 B.C. The Colossus was broken at the knees and toppled to the ground.

People in the ancient world were very sad to see the beautiful statue in ruins.

"Please let me pay to rebuild the monument," said a descendant of Ptolemy.

But the people of Rhodes were not eager to rebuild their precious statue.

"We will be cursed if we rebuild our monument to Helios," they said. They were afraid. So they declined the offer. They let the statue lie where it fell for 800 years.

Then in 653 A.D. Arab pirates were raiding the area.

"Look at all the bronze!" they cried when they discovered the ruins. "We're rich!"

So the pirates broke up the ruins into small pieces. They took the pieces to Syria and sold them as scrap metal.

Legend has it that it took 900 camels to carry away the statue.

THE PLAY

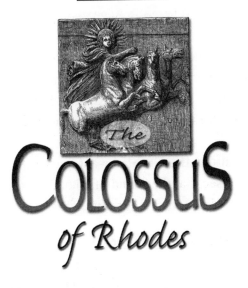

COLOSSUS
of Rhodes

Cast of Characters

Narrator

Alexander the Great

Ptolemy

Seleucus

Antigous

Rhodians

Demetrius

Aegean pirate

Advisor

Rhodian citizen 1

Rhodian citizen 2

Descendant of Ptolemy

Arab pirates

Setting: Island of Rhodes, 324 B.C.

Act One

Narrator: Where the Aegean Sea and the Mediterranean Sea meet is a little island called Rhodes. In ancient times the island had one of the best natural harbors in the area. So in 408 B.C. a city was built. It was called Rhodes. It became important for trading in the ancient world.

Alexander the Great: I want to expand my empire. I see that the island of Rhodes has a good harbor. I will capture it for myself!

Narrator: So in 332 B.C. Alexander the Great took control of the little island. However, he died nine years later. He was only 33. His death caused some squabbling among his generals.

Ptolemy: Now that Alexander is dead, I will control his vast kingdom!

Seleucus: Why should you get to control it? I have just as much right to it as you do!

Antigous: Hey, don't forget about me. Alexander would have wanted me to rule his land!

Narrator: The three generals fought. The fight ended with the kingdom being divided into three parts. But all was not well.

Rhodians: We want Ptolemy! We want Ptolemy!

Antigous: I am angry at those people of Rhodes. They supported Ptolemy during the power struggle. I won this little island. But the people will not listen to me. They will not obey me. They want Ptolemy.

Narrator: Antigous knew he had to do something. He could not have control over an island if the people were loyal to someone else. He got an idea.

Antigous: Demetrius! Demetrius, come here! Oh, where's my son?

Demetrius: Here I am, Father. What is it?

Antigous: There is something I want you to do for me. I am sending you to Rhodes. You must punish the city for me because they are rebelling.

Demetrius: Very well, Father. I will do as you wish.

Act Two

Narrator: Demetrius set off for Rhodes. He took with him an army of 40,000 men. That was even more than the entire population of Rhodes! Along the way, he saw some Aegean pirates.

Demetrius: Hello, there! Would you be interested in a little adventure?

Aegean pirate: Adventure? We're always looking for adventure. What kind of adventure is this?

Demetrius: I am going to invade a city. There will be a lot of fighting, and we could use your help.

Aegean pirate: Well, we're always eager for a good fight. I'll bet there'll be a lot of treasure to loot too. Count us in!

Narrator: When Demetrius, his army, and the pirates arrived, they noticed that the city of Rhodes was surrounded by a tall, strong wall. Little did they know that behind that wall was a city not willing to give up easily.

Demetrius: How do you suggest we get over that wall?

Advisor: I think we should try building a seige tower to climb over it.

Demetrius: Seige tower?

Advisor: It's a wooden structure with armlike catapults. It can be used to scale a wall.

Demetrius: Good idea. Can we bring it in on sea?

Advisor: Well, usually the towers are rolled on land. But we could give the sea a try.

Demetrius: I think it will work if we mount the tower to six ships that are lashed together.

Narrator: However, luck was not on Demetrius's side. As he was getting ready for attack, a storm erupted. The tower was turned over and smashed. The people of Rhodes won the battle.

Demetrius: I'm not ready to give up. Advisor, take notes.

Advisor: Yes, sir.

Demetrius: I want a "supertower" to be built. This one will be 150 feet high. It will have many more catapults. We will cover it with wood and leather to protect the troops inside from flying arrows. It will even carry water tanks. That way we can put out any fires that are started by flaming arrows.

Advisor: Are we going to bring it in on sea again?

Demetrius: No. This one will be on wheels. We can roll it up to the wall.

Advisor: Nothing will stop this supertower!

Narrator: But the people of Rhodes had a different plan.

The army began rolling the big tower up to the wall. They were ready for attack. Arrows began flying, and soldiers were in position to man the catapults. Everything seemed to be going their way.

Demetrius: Wait! What is that rushing noise I hear? It sounds like water!

Advisor: Look, Demetrius! The Rhodians are flooding the ditch outside the wall!

Demetrius: Ooh, I hadn't thought of that.

Advisor: Oh, no! The supertower is sinking in the mud!

Demetrius: Could it get any worse?

Advisor: Yes! Look out to sea! There's a fleet of ships approaching the harbor.

Demetrius: Look at the flags. Can you tell whom they belong to?

Advisor: Yes, they are Ptolemy's. He must've sent them from Egypt to help the people of Rhodes!

Demetrius: Well, it looks like it's all over. I'm not sticking around. Let's get out of here!

Advisor: But what about the supertower?

Demetrius: Just leave it there in the mud. Come on!

Narrator: So Demetrius and his army quickly fled, leaving all their weapons and war machines behind.
The people of Rhodes were so happy to have defeated Demetrius and his army. They were free!

Act Three

Rhodian citizen 1: What should we do to celebrate?

Narrator: Many people had ideas. But one stood out from the rest.

Rhodian citizen 2: I know! Let's build a giant statue of our patron god Helios!

Rhodian citizen 1: Perfect! But what should we use to build it?

Narrator: No one spoke for a moment. They were all thinking. They looked around and saw the seige tower and the other war machines and weapons.

Rhodian citizen 1: We'll melt down the bronze from the war machines!

Rhodian citizen 2: Right! And we'll use the seige tower as the scaffolding while we're building the statue!

Narrator: Construction took 12 years. But when it was finally finished, the statue stood 110 feet high. The figure wore a spiked crown. It shaded its eyes from the rising sun with its right hand. It held a cloak over its left hand. It stood on a 50-foot pedestal near the entrance of the harbor.

The Colossus stood guard over the harbor for only 66 years. A strong earthquake hit Rhodes in 226 B.C. The Colossus was broken at the knees and toppled to the ground.

Descendant of Ptolemy: People from all over the world are very sad to see your beautiful statue in ruins. Please, Rhodians, let me pay to rebuild the statue.

Narrator: But the Rhodians were not eager to rebuild their precious statue.

Rhodians: We will be cursed if we rebuild our monument to Helios! We decline your offer.

Narrator: So they let the statue lie where it fell for 800 years. Then in 653 A.D. Arab pirates were raiding the area.

Arab pirates: Look at all the bronze! We're rich!

Narrator: So the pirates broke up the ruins into small pieces. They took the pieces to Syria and sold them as scrap metal.

Legend has it that it took 900 camels to carry away the statue.